KEN GRIFFEY JR.

BASEBALL'S BEST

BY BILL GUTMAN

Millbrook Sports World
The Millbrook Press
Brookfield, Connecticut

8871584

Cover photographs courtesy of Allsport (© Brian Bahr; inset © Doug Densinger)

Photographs courtesy of AP/Wide World: pp. 3, 4, 18-19, 22, 25, 27, 29, 33, 41, 46; The Cincinnati Reds: p. 8; *The Cincinnati Enquirer*: pp. 9, 11; © Jim Callaway 1987: p. 12; *The Bellingham Herald*: p. 14; Allsport: p. 26 (© Stephen Dunn); The Seattle Mariners: pp. 31, 35; Reuters/Archive Photos: pp. 37 (Ray Stubblebine), 39 (Sue Ogrocki); Rod Mar/*Seattle Times*: p. 43; Steve Crandall & Associates: p. 44

Library of Congress Cataloging-in-Publication Data
Gutman, Bill.
Ken Griffey Jr. : baseball's best / Bill Gutman.
p.   cm. — (Millbrook sports world)
Includes index.
Summary: Highlights the life and career of baseball player Ken Griffey Jr., centerfielder for the Seattle Mariners.
ISBN 0-7613-0415-0 (lib. bdg.). — ISBN 0-7613-0381-2 (pbk.)
1. Griffey, Ken, Jr.—Juvenile literature. 2. Baseball players—United States—Biography—Juvenile literature. 3. Seattle Mariners (Baseball team)—Juvenile literature. [1. Griffey, Ken, Jr. 2. Baseball players. 3. Afro-Americans—Biography.] I. Title. II. Series.
GV865.G69G86 1998
796.357'092—dc21
[B] 97-51679 CIP AC

Published by The Millbrook Press, Inc.
2 Old New Milford Road
Brookfield, Connecticut 06804

KEN GRIFFEY JR.

On April 26, 1990, the Seattle Mariners were playing the New York Yankees at Yankee Stadium in New York City. Early in the game, Yankees right fielder Jesse Barfield came to bat. Barfield had 199 career home runs and was eager to get his 200th.

Out in center field, 20-year-old Ken Griffey Jr. was playing straightaway and medium deep. Griffey Jr. was in his second big-league season and the youngest player in the major leagues. In the eyes of nearly everyone, he was a future superstar. And that night in Yankee Stadium, someone very special to young Griffey was watching the game.

Great catches seem like second nature to Ken Griffey Jr. This one took place at the Seattle Kingdome in 1991. Junior climbed the outfield wall to rob the Rangers' Ruben Sierra.

His father, Ken Griffey Sr., was in New York for the game because his team, the Cincinnati Reds, had an off night. That's right: Both father and son were major-league baseball players. It was the first time in history that a father and son had played in the big leagues at the same time.

But now Barfield was up and Ken Jr. had to concentrate on the game. Sure enough, Barfield got his pitch and slammed a long, high drive toward the left center-field wall. Ken Jr. broke quickly at the crack of the bat and was racing toward the wall at full speed. Would he get there before the ball? And if he did, would he be able to catch it?

He continued his run toward the 8-foot (2.5-meter)- high wall. When he felt the warning track beneath his feet he took a quick look at the wall to judge his distance. Then he started his leap several yards from the wall. Ken Jr. looked almost like a high jumper as he took a huge step, then sank the cleats of his left shoe nearly halfway up the wall. He went as high as he could.

The pitchers in the Seattle bullpen behind the wall saw an arm rise high above the wall. The arm snapped back over the top just as Barfield's long drive began falling behind the wall. The pitchers saw Ken Jr.'s arm whiplash back out of sight, bringing the ball with it.

It had been an incredible catch. For a split second, Yankees fans were almost stunned to silence. Ken Jr. simply trotted toward the infield as if the catch had been routine. Then the applause began to build. Everyone in the ballpark knew they had just seen something remarkable.

"As I jumped, I thought I had a chance," Ken Jr. would say later. "It's probably the best catch I ever made. It's the first one I've caught going over the wall, in practice or a game."

It wouldn't be long before baseball fans all over the country would get used to seeing amazing things from Ken Griffey Jr.: great catches, long home runs, clutch throws. These were all part of his game.

His father, a fine ballplayer in his own right, was happy to witness his son's superb catch. "I'm in awe of him the same as you guys are," Ken Sr. told the press. "Yes, I'm a very proud dad."

FOLLOWING IN LARGE FOOTSTEPS

Ken Griffey Jr. was born on November 21, 1969, in Donora, Pennsylvania. That put him in position to continue a baseball tradition. Ken Sr. had also been born in Donora, and so had one of the sport's greatest players, Stan Musial.

Musial was born in 1920 and went on to a Hall of Fame career with the St. Louis Cardinals. One of Musial's teammates at Donora High School was Buddy Griffey. A left-handed-throwing third baseman, Buddy would later become the father of Ken Griffey Sr. who was born in 1950. Ken Sr. also was a fine athlete, starring in football, baseball, and track at Donora High. Then, in the 1969 Major League Baseball draft, the Cincinnati Reds took him in the 29th round.

By the time he was picked by the Reds, Ken and his wife, Alberta, were expecting their first child. When Ken Jr. was born that November, his father was just beginning to work his way through the minor leagues. The Griffeys had a second son, Craig, who was born in June 1971.

In 1973, when Junior was just three years old, Ken Sr. made his big-league debut with the Reds. But he always cherished his years in the minors because it gave the family a chance to be very close.

"[The days] in the minor leagues were the best times," Ken Sr. said, "because that's when I developed a closeness with [my sons]. I was always with them. I had them all the time."

After two years as a part-time player, Ken Sr. became Cincinnati's regular right fielder in 1975. He was on his way to becoming a superior big-league ballplayer. And he was also playing on the most powerful team of the 1970s.

When your father is a major leaguer, you become part of a baseball family. Here the Griffeys gather at Riverfront Stadium in Cincinnati for a family picture. Left to right are Craig; Ken Sr.; Alberta; and Ken Jr. The boys are wearing their dad's number, 30.

Known as the "Big Red Machine," the Cincinnati club won back-to-back World Series in 1975 and 1976.

The team featured players like Pete Rose, Johnny Bench, Tony Perez, Joe Morgan, George Foster, Dave Concepcion, and Cesar Geronimo. Ken Griffey Sr. was part of one of the most powerful lineups in baseball history. Ken was 5 feet 11 (180 centimeters) and a solid 190 pounds (86 kilograms). He hit line drives to all fields and was very fast on the bases and in the outfield.

This was the baseball atmosphere that Ken Jr. saw firsthand as a young boy. He spent a great deal of time at Riverfront Stadium in Cincinnati, where he not only met the players but made friends with their sons, as well. He often played catch with Pete Rose Jr., Eduardo and Victor Perez, Lee May Jr., and Brian McRae. As a group, the boys were often called the "Little Red Machine."

Ken Jr. developed a feel for the game of baseball at an early age. When he was just 6 years old, he watched his father play winter ball in Puerto Rico. After

Ken Sr. struck out, young Ken yelled, "That pitcher's got nothing." He was trying to encourage his father. But when the elder Griffey struck out a second time, his son shouted, "Dad, *you* got nothing."

It was a funny moment they could all laugh about. Ken Sr. would hit over .300 for the Reds in three of the next five years. During that time, Junior began to grow tall and play many sports, especially baseball. He played organized ball for the first time in the summer of 1980. It was in a summer recreation league, for a team sponsored by A & A Janitorial Service.

Ken Jr. was just 10 years old, but he was already a superior player. Parents of players on the other teams thought he was older and didn't want him to play. It got so bad that Alberta Griffey had to bring his birth certificate to every game to prove he was just 10. He was already the team's best hitter and best pitcher. He could also play every position in the field.

At the age of eight, Ken Jr. was a star pitcher and outfielder for the Mt. Airy D-1 team in Cincinnati, Ohio.

Soon people would realize that Ken Griffey Jr. was an outstanding young player who would keep getting better. He had already made up his mind to follow in his father's footsteps.

They were large footsteps, indeed, but Junior would soon prove that his were even larger.

BECOMING A NUMBER-ONE PICK

Ken Griffey Sr.'s career may have reached its apex in the 1980 All-Star Game. He whacked a home run and was named the game's Most Valuable Player. After 1981, however, life changed for the Griffey family. Ken Sr. was traded to the New York Yankees during the off-season. Because the rest of the family remained in Cincinnati, Ken Sr. had to be apart from them much of the time. He wasn't home during the baseball season, so he didn't see his eldest son play very often. Junior was growing taller and stronger, and becoming an even better player. Even though Ken Sr. could not be there, Junior always knew that Dad was just a phone call away.

"If I needed to talk to him, I would call him after the game," Junior said. "If I did something wrong [on the field] Dad would sometimes fly me to New York and tell me what I should have done. Then he would send me home the next day, and I'd play baseball."

In the fall of 1983, Junior entered Moeller High School in Cincinnati as a freshman. He would star in both baseball and football. For three years he was a hard-hitting outfielder on the baseball team, and a speedy tailback and acrobatic wide receiver for the football team. In fact, since his father was always home during football season, Ken Sr. thought his son's future might be on the gridiron.

In the summer of 1986, when Junior was 16, he began playing in the Connie Mack League. An amateur league, it had teams all around the country. It is named

after a Baseball Hall of Famer who managed the Philadelphia Athletics for 50 years. Junior showed that he was more than ready to play with older kids by leading his team to the Connie Mack World Series. In the Series he hit three long home runs. One was to left field, one to center, and the other to right.

As a split-end and tailback on the Moeller High School football team in Cincinnati, Junior was so outstanding that even his father thought he had a future on the gridiron.

Even as a high school athlete, Junior had all the tools—he could hit, run, and throw. Intensity shows in his eyes, the eyes of a future major-leaguer.

That fall, Junior made a big decision. He decided not to play football as a high school senior so he could concentrate on baseball. There was no doubt now what he wanted to do.

That spring, big-league scouts flocked to Moeller High to see him play. He was already taller than his father, standing 6 feet 3 inches (190 centimeters) and weighing 195 pounds (88 kilograms). Like his father, Junior was a left-handed hitter. He had a big, smooth power stroke that could send the ball a long way.

Just one situation made Junior nervous: the rare occasions when his father came to watch him play.

"When he [Griffey Sr.] was there, it was the only time I thought I had to impress somebody," Junior said. "But he'd tell me he was the one guy I *didn't* have to impress."

Not surprisingly, Junior had a superb senior year at Moeller. After the baseball season he was named Player of the Year in the conference for the second-straight time. He looked close to being ready for the majors, and the scouts knew it, too. When the 1987 Major League draft rolled around in June, Ken

Griffey Jr. became the first player chosen by the Seattle Mariners, who had the first pick overall. There was no doubt that he was the best player available.

MINOR LEAGUES, MAJOR CRISIS

Just a few days after graduating from Moeller High School at age 17, Ken Griffey Jr. became a professional baseball player when he signed a contract with the Mariners. Like most young players, Junior had to start in the minor leagues. The Mariners sent him to their Class A minor-league team in Bellingham, Washington. Bellingham was in the Northwest League and played a short season, giving the young ballplayers a chance to get used to life as professionals. The town was located 90 miles (145 kilometers) north of Seattle, Washington, and just 20 miles (32 kilometers) from the Canadian border.

On the field, Junior quickly showed that he belonged. His first professional home run came on June 17, against the Everett Giants. That week he hit 3 more homers, drove in 8 runs, and stole 4 bases. For his efforts, he was named Northwest League Player of the Week.

Off the field, however, it wasn't as easy. Junior was finding those adjustments much tougher. For one thing, there were very few black people in Bellingham. That may have made him feel uncomfortable. "Things are a little different here," he admitted. "It will take some getting used to for me. But I have to mature. That's why I'm here."

But the problems continued. The team had to travel up to ten hours in an old school bus with no bathroom facilities. To make matters worse, two local teenage boys began harassing Junior, calling him cruel names. One of them even threatened to come after him with a gun. These problems and a strong case of homesickness made Junior sometimes want to call it quits.

Junior began his minor-league career at Bellingham, Washington, in the Northwest League. Though he still had the look of a teenager, his big-league potential was very obvious.

This period of adjustment also led to an old-fashioned batting slump. But after sitting out a week with a shoulder injury, he came back and caught fire. From July 12 to August 13, 1987, Junior hit .453 with 7 homers and 16 runs batted in. And when the season ended he had a solid .313 average in 54 games, as well as a team-leading 14 home runs, 40 RBIs, and 13 stolen bases.

After the season he was named to the all-league team and also voted the top major-league prospect in the Northwest League by the publication *Baseball*

America. Despite a rocky start, he had put together an outstanding first professional season.

Before returning home, Junior spent some time in the Instructional League in Arizona working on the fundamentals of the game. But instead of a happy homecoming in Cincinnati that fall, Ken Griffey Jr. suddenly found himself dealing with the biggest crisis of his life.

For the first time, Junior and his father weren't getting along. "Dad wanted me to pay rent or get my own place," said Junior. "I was confused and hurting. It seemed like everyone was yelling at me in baseball. Then, when I came home everyone was yelling at me there. I got depressed. I got angry. I didn't want to live."

Ken Sr. was probably trying to teach his son responsibility. After all, Junior was now earning a living as a professional athlete. But Junior had just come through a difficult season and was looking forward to returning home where things would be as they had been before. Suddenly he felt in turmoil.

One day in January 1988, Junior was with his girlfriend and her brother. He was still depressed. He grabbed a large bottle of aspirin and swallowed all of it. His friends tried to stop him but couldn't. Soon, he became sick. His girlfriend's mother drove him quickly to a nearby hospital. There, doctors pumped his stomach and put him in intensive care.

When Ken Sr. heard what had happened he became very frightened. He was also angry that his son would do such a thing. He rushed to the hospital, and as soon as he saw his son the two got into another argument.

"I ripped the IV out of my arm," Junior remembered. "That stopped him from yelling."

Finally, both father and son realized that they had major problems. They resolved those problems through long, heart-to-heart talks. They not only talked about the things that were bothering them but also about all the good times they had had. They continued talking right up until both left for spring training.

At the time of the incident, no one outside the family and a few friends knew about it. But in 1992, Junior and his family decided to make the story public. He first told it to a newspaper reporter in Seattle. Junior said he was going public with the hope that his story might prevent other teenagers from seeing suicide as a solution to their problems.

Fortunately, both father and son continued to communicate and to develop a positive relationship. And once Junior got back on the diamond for the 1988 season, he really began to make his mark.

YOUNGEST PLAYER IN THE MAJORS

In 1988, Junior divided his time between the Class A San Bernadino Spirit of the California League and the Class AA Burlington Mariners of Vermont in the Eastern League. He hit .338 in 58 games at San Bernadino, with 11 homers and 42 RBIs. He would have had even better numbers if he had not suffered a back injury diving for a ball in the outfield. He was on the disabled list for two months.

When he came off the DL he moved on to Vermont. There, he hit just .279 in 17 games, his back injury limiting him to designated hitter duties. But in the Eastern League playoffs he hit .444 with 8 hits in 18 at bats and a club-best 7 RBIs. He finished the season on a high note.

Like many top prospects, Junior was invited to the Seattle Mariners training camp. The general opinion was that Junior would probably need another full year in the minors at the Triple-A level. But when Mariners manager Jim Lefebvre saw Junior's natural talent for the first time, he made a quick decision. He would play Junior in center field every day during spring training. "I want to take a good look at him," the manager said. "Then we'll see how it goes."

So Junior went out and played. He appeared completely relaxed, and his talent showed. Once he began hitting he didn't stop. The more Manager Lefebvre looked at Junior, the more he wanted to see. At one point in the exhibition season the young phenom had a 15-game hitting streak. During a three-week stretch of games he never went more than four at-bats without getting a hit.

He was just as good in the field. In a game against the San Francisco Giants, Junior cut down the speedy Brett Butler, who was trying to go from first to third base on a single. Young Griffey charged the ball and fired a strike to third. The ball never touched the ground.

About a week before the regular season was to begin, Lefebvre called Junior to his office. Junior thought he was about to be sent down to Triple-A. Instead, he received news of a different kind.

"Congratulations," his manager said. "You're my starting center fielder."

For Junior, it was a dream come true. For a moment he couldn't say a word. "When he said that, my heart started ticking again," he remembered. "Those were probably the best words I've ever heard."

Since Ken Sr. was still an active player, some skeptics thought that Junior was being kept with the Mariners so the Griffeys could become the first father and son to play in the majors at the same time. Manager Lefebvre just scoffed at those rumors.

"It's a good story," the manager said. "But I didn't bring [Junior] onto this ball club because he's a good story. He earned a spot here. He outplayed a lot of people for that spot."

The numbers backed up Lefebvre's statement. For the spring, Junior hit a sizzling .360 while setting Seattle preseason records with 32 hits, 49 total bases, and 20 runs batted in. He certainly had earned his spot.

When the 1989 season opened, 19-year-old Ken Griffey Jr. took his place in center field for the Mariners. He was the youngest player in the major leagues. In addition, he and his father *did* make history as the first father and son to play in the majors at the same time. That was something that made them both proud. But Junior also knew that there would be comparisons.

"It's harder being a baseball player when your father is a baseball player," he said. "People will say, 'Your dad hit .300 lifetime, so you have to hit .310

As a 19-year-old rookie in 1989, Junior was the youngest player in the majors. A year later, he was still the youngest but already playing like a veteran. Here, he tracks down a long drive by Mike Greenwell of the Boston Red Sox.

to be better.' They put you in a category with your father, and that's not fair because you are two different people."

Junior started to prove this difference right away. In his first at bat, against top right-handed pitcher Dave Stewart of the Oakland A's, Junior smacked a line drive off the right-field wall for a double. A week later, in his first at bat before the hometown fans at the Seattle Kingdome, he slammed his first major-league homer, an opposite field shot off Eric King of the Chicago White Sox.

Junior was off and running. By the All-Star break at midseason he was hitting a solid .279 with 13 homers and 38 RBIs. He seemed well on his way to a great rookie season. But then, after a game with the White Sox on July 24, Junior slipped while stepping out of the shower in his hotel room. He tried to break his fall with his right hand. In doing so, he fractured a bone that ran from his wrist to his little finger. The next day he was placed on the disabled list and learned that he would be out for a month.

At the time of his injury Junior's batting average was up to .287. Many felt he had a good chance to hit .300. But when he returned to the lineup in August, something had changed. He seemed to be trying too hard. "He was trying to catch up with the other Rookie of the Year candidates with one swing," said Manager Lefebvre. "He just lost his poise."

Even Junior admitted that he had made a mistake. "I was worrying about hitting the ball 700 feet," he said. "I just wanted 20 home runs."

Despite his slump, Junior finished his rookie year with a .264 batting average in 127 games. He also had 23 doubles, 16 home runs, and 61 runs batted in. There have been better rookie seasons, but Junior was still just 19 years old. There wasn't a person in baseball who didn't feel Ken Griffey Jr. would soon become a superstar.

A HISTORIC MOMENT

Still the youngest player in the majors in 1990, Junior started the season on a tear. At one point early in the year he was leading the league in hitting and was near the top in home runs and runs batted in. Then in a late-April game at Yankee Stadium, he made his great leaping catch on the home-run bid by Jesse Barfield. That one made all the highlight films.

"Every time he makes one of those plays, you think he'll never top it," said Manager Lefebvre. "You can't believe how much it picks up the entire club. He's going to be one of the real marquee players in this league."

By the All-Star break in 1990, Junior was showing signs of fulfilling all the predictions. He was hitting .331 with 12 homers and 40 RBIs. He was also leading the American League with 107 hits. To top it off, he was voted the starting center fielder on the American League All-Star team.

By mid-August he was hitting .323 with 16 homers and 56 RBIs. As a team, the Mariners were trying to finish at .500 or better, with at least as many wins as losses. Formed in 1977, Seattle had not yet achieved a winning season.

On August 18, Ken Griffey Sr. who was now back with the Cincinnati Reds, was placed on waivers. The Reds wanted to make room for a younger player. That meant that any club could claim the 40-year-old veteran. To the surprise of many, it was the Mariners who claimed him.

At first, it was thought that Seattle had taken Ken Sr. as a publicity stunt. If you put a father and son together on a team, it was reasoned, the fans would flock to see baseball history in the making. But Manager Lefebvre said that this wasn't the reason. The Mariners felt that the elder Griffey could still play. "[Ken Griffey Sr.] is here to make a contribution on the field and in the clubhouse," Lefebvre said.

Ken Sr. was still playing baseball when Junior joined the Mariners in 1989. The next year, the Griffeys made more history when they became teammates on the Mariners. Interviews like this became commonplace for the first father and son to play both in the majors at the same time and *on the same team.*

On the night of August 31, more than 27,000 fans were at the Kingdome. Number 30 trotted out to left field for the Mariners, while number 24 jogged out to center field. Separated by nearly 20 years in age, father and son were in the same outfield trying to do the same thing—help win a baseball game for their team.

Early in the game, Griffey Sr. made a beautiful play, taking a hit by speedy Bo Jackson off the left-field wall and firing a strike to second base to nab the sliding Jackson.

In center field, Junior was grinning from ear to ear. "It runs in the family," he shouted to his father.

After the game, a cluster of reporters gathered around the two Griffeys. Junior looked at the lighter side of the historic occasion. "It seemed like a father-son game," he said, "like we were out in the backyard playing catch."

But his father couldn't help talking about how much playing alongside his son meant to him. "You can talk about the two World Series I played in, and the All-Star games," he said. "But this is number one. This is the best thing that's ever happened to me. This is the pinnacle."

Ken Sr. wound up playing 21 games for the Mariners, hitting a solid .377 with 3 homers and 18 RBIs. Manager Lefebvre had been right. The veteran could still play and contribute. As for Junior, he put together a fine second season. Despite a slight letdown in the final months, he wound up hitting an even .300 with 22 homers and 80 runs batted in. The team finished at 77-85, but with some promising young players and the two Griffeys, the Mariners hoped to improve in 1991.

A TRUE SUPERSTAR

The 1991 season would be the last for Ken Griffey Sr. An auto accident in March resulted in back and neck injuries that kept him out of the lineup for the first couple of weeks. But by the end of April he was back and hitting .308. Then, in June, he had to go back on the disabled list with a ruptured disk in his neck. At the age of 41, it was thought that his career might be over.

Junior had a hot start, but then slumped. By the All-Star Game in July he was hitting just .281 with 9 homers. But he was voted a starter again and had two hits in a 4-2 American League victory. After the All-Star break he caught fire and began hitting as well as anyone in the league. He hit .410 in July and .377 in August.

Junior was doing it all. At the age of 21, he was a complete ballplayer. What's more, he was helping his team win. When the season ended, the Mariners had their first winning record in their 14-year history, 83-79. And Junior finished with his best season ever. He batted .327 with 22 home runs and 100 runs batted in. In December, he received a second-straight Gold Glove award as the best defensive player at his position.

During his first three seasons Junior's batting average had gone from .264 to .300 to .327. That made him the first player in baseball history to increase his average by 25 points or more in each of his first three seasons. He had already become a true superstar.

Ken Sr. announced his retirement shortly after having surgery for his neck injury. In 19 big-league seasons, Ken Griffey Sr. had achieved a lifetime batting average of .296. It was a very solid career. Now he could watch his son become one of the best of *his* generation—and maybe one of the best ever.

Junior continued to show he was one of baseball's leaders in 1992. He batted .308 with a career best 27 homers and 103 runs batted in. Once again he was an All-Star starter. This time he belted a home run off Greg Maddox of the Chicago Cubs, had two other hits, and was named the game's Most Valuable Player. At season's end, he won his third-straight Gold Glove prize.

In 1993 the Mariners got a new manager. Lou Piniella, who had been a respected player and had managed the Yankees and then the Cincinnati Reds, took over the team. Seattle was also adding some fine players to their lineup, such as third baseman Edgar Martinez, first baseman Tino Martinez, outfielder Jay Buhner, and pitcher Randy Johnson.

Junior's long, smooth, and powerful swing was a thing of beauty, something that couldn't be taught. It wasn't surprising that as he matured, his power and home-run numbers increased.

Junior came into the new season a different man. During the winter he had been married. He had met his wife, Melissa, several years earlier at a dance held at an under-21 club, which both Junior and Melissa liked because it was alcohol-free. Junior was ready to have a big year, and that's just what happened. He had been a .300 hitter most of his career, but in 1993 he blossomed into a big-time slugger. On May 9, he blasted a 460-foot (140-meter) homer off Scott Erickson (of the Minnesota Twins). On June 15, he became the sixth-youngest player in baseball history to reach 100 career home runs.

On July 18, he set a new record for American League outfielders by handling 542 chances without making an error. He would run the record streak to 573 before finally committing a miscue. In late July he tied another major-league mark by hitting home runs in eight-straight games. Yet he was never one to talk about setting records. "I don't play to break records," he said. "I play to win ball games. I'm happier with a game-winning single than a home run if we lose."

Junior (left) stops for a chat with the Giants' Barry Bonds during spring training in 1993. The two outfielders were widely considered the best all-around players in baseball.

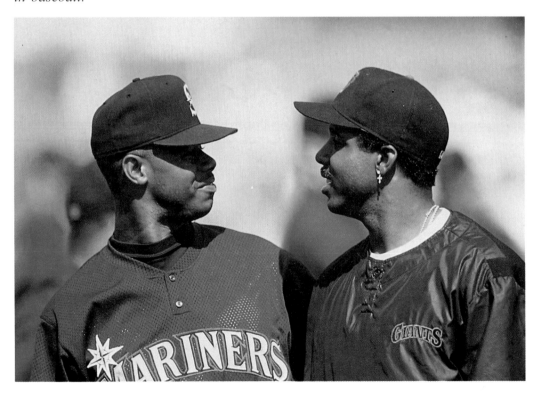

Though Junior had filled out to a solid 205 pounds (93 kilograms), he still didn't look like a typical big home-run hitter. It was his quickness and picture-perfect swing that enabled him to drive the ball. "You don't really have to be strong," he said. "You have to be quick. You have to trust your hands. If you can keep your eye on the ball as it leaves the pitcher's hand, your hands will automatically take you where the ball is going."

The Mariners finished the year with an 82-80 record. Edgar Martinez was hurt a good part of the year, but Randy Johnson won 19 games, while Jay Buhner hit 27 homers and drove home 98 runs. The team's big star, however, was Ken Griffey Jr. In 1993, Junior hit .309 with 45 homers and 109 RBIs. He was just one home run

Junior acknowledges a cheering Seattle crowd in September 1993. The local baseball writers had just honored him as the Mariners' Most Valuable Player. He hit a career-high 45 home runs that year.

behind Barry Bonds of the San Francisco Giants and Juan Gonzalez of the Texas Rangers for the major-league home-run lead. He was voted by the players to the *Sporting News* All-Star team and won a fourth-straight Gold Glove. In the eyes of many, he had become the best all-around player in the game.

During the off-season, Junior faced a new challenge, but a very happy one. On January 19, 1994, his son, Trey Kenneth Griffey, was born.

"Every day I pinch myself and say I can't believe I have a baby," he said. "He's mine. You could take away baseball, take away all the material things, but I would still have him. That means everything to me."

Having a son gave him some new skills to master. "Changing diapers, now that's rough," he kidded. "When I change his diaper he picks up one leg, and when I push it down, he picks up the other. It's hard work. He's so little. I just don't want to drop him and break him."

During the off-season, Junior also had a part in a movie called "Little Big League." According to the movie's director, Junior was a natural at acting as well. But now the important thing was to get back to baseball and try to help push the Mariners to the next level.

A WINNING TEAM

By 1994, Junior was perhaps the best player in the game. He was also becoming the most popular. He had a friendly smile for anyone and was always ready to sign autographs for kids. He spent his time off the field with his new family.

On the field, it was apparent that Junior was better than ever. He was belting the ball all over the lot, and for distance. By the end of April he had set a club record with 20 runs batted in. On May 24, he became the third-youngest player ever to reach 150 career home runs. The only problem was that the Mariners weren't winning. That's what bothered Junior the most.

"[Building a winning team] is always out of my hands," he said. "That's the frustrating thing. If some of the guys around here don't improve, they won't be here next year. That's the way the game is, and that's how it has to be."

At the All-Star break, Junior was hitting .329 with 33 home runs and 69 runs batted in. There was talk of him breaking the record of 61 homers in a

Junior blasts the second of two homers against the Kansas City Royals in May 1994. When the season was ended by a players' strike in August, Junior was leading the league with 40 homers in 111 games. Had there been no strike, he might have had a chance to break the all-time record of 61.

single season. He also received an all-time record 6,079,688 votes for the All-Star team. His popularity was enormous.

But as Junior racked up incredible numbers, trouble was brewing elsewhere in baseball. The Players' Union and baseball team owners had been trying to work out a new contract. They couldn't agree. Finally, the players threatened to strike. There had been a number of strikes before. Most didn't last long, and usually happened at the beginning or in the middle of the season. This one was called to begin after the games of August 11.

Sure enough, there were no games on August 12. Almost everyone thought that the strike would last a week or two at the most, but the two sides couldn't come to an agreement. On September 14, the unthinkable happened. With no agreement in sight, the remainder of the 1994 baseball season was canceled. There would be no playoffs, no World Series. The big losers were the fans.

Another one who lost out was Ken Griffey Jr. He had been on his way to an outstanding season. In 111 games, Junior hit a solid .323. He led the American League with 40 home runs and drove home 90 runs. Over a full season, his numbers could have been record-breaking.

Another disappointment was the team record. The Mariners finished at 49-63. In some ways, that bothered Junior more than the strike and his lost season. As he had said more than once, "I don't play to break records; I play for the Seattle Mariners."

The longest strike in professional sports history lasted 234 days. It even cut into the beginning of the 1995 season. The late start would limit the season to 144 games, 18 fewer than usual. This time the Mariners were really under pressure to become a winner. Attendance by the fans was down, and there was talk of the team being sold, maybe even moved out of Seattle.

Junior started quickly, then slumped in May. Everyone was waiting for him to go on one of his batting tears—he was due for one. On the night of May 26, the Mariners were hosting the Baltimore Orioles at the Kingdome. When Baltimore's Kevin Bass hit a long drive to deep right-center field, Junior gave chase at full speed, heading for the wall. At the last second, he reached across his body with his right arm, stretched as far as he could, and made another brilliant catch. Then he crashed into the wall, trying to brace himself with his left hand. He trotted off the field in obvious pain and had to leave the game.

An examination later revealed that Junior had fractured both bones in his left wrist. It was a very serious injury, especially for a hitter who depended on quick and strong wrists for his power. The next day Junior underwent three hours of surgery. Doctors had to put a 4-inch (10-centimeter) metal plate and seven screws in the wrist to hold the bones in place. Junior was expected to be out of the Mariners lineup for three months.

At the time of his injury, Junior was hitting just .263 with 7 homers and 15 RBIs in 27 games. That was below his usual pace. Now he had to sit out, something he never liked. "Naturally, I'm disappointed," he said. "I feel I'm letting everyone down by not being able to play. I'll just have to . . . try to rehab the wrist as fast as I can."

He did rehabilitate quickly, returning on August 15, two weeks ahead of schedule. By that time, however, the Mariners were hovering around the .500

By 1995, Junior was one of the best, and also one of the most popular, players in baseball. Here he spends some time making a youngster's wish to meet him come true. It was part of his work with the Make-A-Wish Foundation.

mark and were 12 ½ games behind the California Angels in the American League Western Division.

By August 24, the Mariners were just 54-55 and facing the New York Yankees. The Yanks had a 7-6 lead as Seattle batted in the bottom of the ninth inning. New York relief ace John Wetteland was on the mound trying to close it out. He got the first two Mariners batters out before Vince Coleman walked, then stole second and third. A single by Joey Cora drove Coleman home with the tying run. Now Junior stepped up to the plate.

Wetteland tried to slip an inside fastball past him, but Junior turned on it. The ball was hit high and deep to right field. Junior knew that it was a home run. He threw his arms in the air and watched the ball sail into the seats. Then he circled the bases to a thunderous ovation. The Mariners had won the game 8-6. It seemed as if Junior's hit had turned the whole season around.

From that point on, the Mariners stayed hot. By September 21, they had won 22 of their last 29 games and had moved past the Angels into first place. The Angels didn't quit, either, and the two teams wound up tied for first with identical 78-66 records. They had to meet in a one-game playoff to determine the division winner and which team would go to the playoffs.

For the Mariners, big Randy Johnson was on the pitcher's mound and completely dominated the Angels. The Mariners won it, 9-1, for their first ever division title. The win also gave Johnson an amazing 18-2 record for the year.

Because of his wrist injury, Junior played in just 72 games in 1995. He hit a career-low .258, but managed 17 homers and 42 RBIs. Fortunately, the Mariners got a lot of hitting from Jay Buhner, Edgar and Tino Martinez, Mike Blowers, and others. In the playoffs, however, Ken Griffey Jr. stepped up.

In 1995 the "wild card" team (the one with the best second-place record) was introduced. That made for an extra playoff series prior to the League Championship Series and the World Series. The Mariners met the wild card New York

Yankees in a best-of-five series. The New Yorkers won the first two games at Yankee Stadium before the Mariners rallied to win the next three at the Kingdome and advance to the American League Championship Series.

Junior was brilliant in the five games. With the metal plate and surgical screws in his wrist, he walloped a record 5 home runs and had 9 hits in the series. He batted a sizzling .391 and drove home 7 runs. Now the Mariners had to go up against the Cleveland Indians in a best-of-seven series to see which team would move on to the World Series.

Unfortunately, the Mariners finally ran out of miracles. Randy Johnson seemed tired, and Junior's bat cooled somewhat. Edgar Martinez, who had also helped blast the Yankees, was not effective against the Indians. Cleveland won the series in six games. Junior hit .333, but had just a single homer and two RBIs.

Although he missed several months of the 1995 season with a broken wrist, Junior still went all out in every phase of the game. Here he slides hard into home while trying to score in a game against the Red Sox.

"We hung in as long as we could," Junior said, afterward. "We just picked the wrong time to stop hitting."

But the Mariners had finally proven that they could win. Junior wanted nothing more than to stay healthy. His morale got a boost that October when his daughter, Taryn Kennedy Griffey, was born. That made losing the American League Championship a little easier to take.

RISING TO THE TOP

Two things kept the 1996 Mariners teams from reaching the playoffs again. Pitching ace Randy Johnson missed nearly the entire season after back surgery. And Junior was out for 20 games with yet another wrist injury. Despite this, however, the Mariners had the best hitting team in the major leagues.

The Mariners finished the 1996 season with an 85-76 record, but were 4½ games behind the division-winning Texas Rangers and 2½ games shy of the wild-card spot. Yet they had had record attendance at the Kingdome and led the American League in runs scored, total bases, doubles, and runs batted in. Their 245 team home runs broke the old record of 240 set by the 1961 New York Yankees.

There were some notable individual performances, as well. Alex Rodriguez, their 20-year-old shortstop, led the American League in batting with a .358 average, slammed 36 homers, and drove home 123 runs. Edgar Martinez hit .327 with 26 homers and 103 RBIs. Jay Buhner walloped 44 homers and drove home 138 runs, both career bests.

Despite missing 20 games with his second broken wrist, Junior still hit a solid .303. Better than that, he amassed a career-best 49 home runs and had 140 RBIs. Playing in just 140 games, he became the ninth major leaguer since 1940 to have driven home a run per game. But when it was mentioned to Junior that if

Many people believe that Junior is baseball's best hope of winning back its young fans. He's never too busy to talk to kids.

he hadn't missed those games he probably would have led the league in homers and RBIs, he just scoffed.

"People don't understand," he said. "I'm not a records guy. I don't pay attention to that. . . . My thing is if I can win a championship. My dad has three of them. I'd like to end my career with one."

Coming into the 1997 season, Ken Griffey Jr. was considered to be baseball's best ambassador as well as the best all-around player in the game. Baseball had never seemed to fully recover from the strike of 1994. With more night games than ever, young kids were watching less baseball and losing inter-est. Because of free agency, players jumped from team to team, going to the highest bidder. Team loyalty was a thing of the past. And many wealthy stars were surly and unfriendly. They even charged money for autographs.

Junior, however, was a breath of fresh air. Although he had a multimillion-dollar contract, he was still a kid at heart and related to kids better than anyone. That kind of thing led one writer to comment: "Ken Griffey Jr. represents baseball's last hope. It goes beyond home runs and history. It's about a friendly nod, a wink or wave, simple courtesy and kindness. . . . This is what separates Griffey [from other superstars], what makes him seem human in an elitist world, what makes him the best candidate for baseball's savior."

Fellow players and fans saw those same qualities in action. Mariners backup catcher John Marsano put it this way: "He's good people. I've seen him spend two hours before a game taking kids in wheelchairs around, showing them his locker, signing stuff for them, hanging out like their old friends."

One 14-year-old from Detroit went to Tigers games only when the Seattle Mariners came to town. His reason was simple: "If the Kid [Junior] wasn't here, we wouldn't be here," he said. "He's just nice. He's always having fun. He plays with the crowd. He says 'hi' to us. Everyone else, they're just like all business. He's more childlike. He's like us."

"Hustle" is Junior's middle name. He plays the game hard day in and day out. If he's not hitting a home run or making a great catch, he might be legging out an infield hit, as he does here against the New York Yankees.

Junior found other ways to give back to the fans, as well. Beginning in 1994, he sponsored Christmas dinners for 350 youngsters from the Rainier Vista Boys and Girls Clubs. And in January 1996, he started the Junior's Kids Center program, which provides free tickets for underprivileged children to all Mariners Saturday night games. He has also won several awards in honor of his "caring for fellow citizens."

What Junior wanted most in 1997, however, was to stay healthy for the entire season. Jumping off to a great start, he was red hot from the opening game. When he smacked 13 home runs in April, he had set a new mark for baseball's opening month. Homer number 12 was also the 250th of his career. Only three other players in baseball history—Jimmie Foxx, Eddie Mathews, and Mel Ott—had reached that mark at an earlier age.

Better yet, the Mariners jumped into first place in the American League West. Everything was on track. When Junior cracked another 11 homers in May, it gave him a total of 24, the most ever at that point in the season. Now there was still more talk about him breaking the record of 61. Reporters asked him the same questions over and over again. But he always kept his cool and answered politely.

Junior's home-run pace slowed in June. He hit just 5, giving him 29 by month's end. Once again he was the leading vote-getter for the All-Star Game. July wasn't a good homer month, either. He slammed number 30 on July 5 and didn't get number 31 until July 25. Talk of record-breaking diminished. But the Mariners still led the West, and that's what the team wanted most—to get back to the playoffs.

By the end of July, Junior had 32 homers. He now trailed the Oakland A's Mark McGwire, who had 34. But on July 31, McGwire was traded to the St. Louis Cardinals of the National League. His total would still count toward the record, but now Junior had the American League to himself. Fans would watch both sluggers closely for the rest of the season.

MOST VALUABLE PLAYER

In August 1997, Junior suddenly found his home-run stroke again. He slammed another dozen shots to bring his total for the year to 44. Two more homers on September 2 gave him 46. With 24 games remaining, Junior needed 16 homers to break the record. It wouldn't be easy. In addition, the Mariners were still in a race with the Angels, leading them by just two games. Every game counted for something.

On September 4, Junior crashed another pair of homers against the Minnesota Twins. The next night he belted number 49 in a 10-6 Mari-

Junior joins the Dodgers' Mike Piazza to display the trophies they won after receiving the most votes from each league prior to the 1997 All-Star Game. Junior had received the top vote in the American League for several years.

ners win. He had tied his career best of a year earlier. He also had 8 homers in his last 11 games. He needed 12 in the final 21 games to break the record. Could he do it?

On Sunday, September 7, Junior whacked his 50th home run. It was a new career high and made him the 15th major-league player to reach that number. But Junior wasn't the only one making a run at the record. Mark McGwire, who had hit 52 the year before, had also blasted his 50th. McGwire, of course, had done it with two teams. He wouldn't lead either league in homers, but he could still break the overall record.

Junior went seven games without another homer. Then he hit two in the next game to give him 52 for the year. By this time, McGwire had 53. The two sluggers continued to run neck and neck. On September 19, Junior belted his 53rd, while McGwire hit his 54th. As much as Junior tried to ignore the home-run race, he admitted that it wasn't easy.

"Did I know Mark hit one today?" he asked himself. "There were 16,000 fans [at Oakland] out there telling me that every inning. But I don't think [McGwire] pays much attention to me, and my job is to help us win games, not catch him."

In a game against Oakland on September 22, Junior did it again. He slammed a line drive just inside the right-field foul pole for homer number 54. And later in the game he hit a mammoth 425-footer to dead center field. He now had 55 home runs with five games left. But when he didn't hit one in the next two games, he finally admitted his chase was over.

"Do I have a chance to break the record?" Junior repeated a reporter's question. "I've got six [homers] to go, and there isn't any way I'm going to break it. The fans may not understand it, but that's the way it is. I keep telling everyone the record's not important. What's important is getting the trophy with all the flags on it [the World Series trophy]. This is a team game, not a one-man show."

Junior would hit one more home run to finish the season with a total of 56. McGwire wound up with 58 (34 with Oakland; 24 with St. Louis). But the over-

More high fives for Junior. This one came after he belted his 54th home run of the 1997 season on September 22, at Oakland. He would finish his greatest year to date with 56 homers and the American League's Most Valuable Player award.

all season put together by Ken Griffey Jr. made him the leader in almost every other way. Playing in 157 games, Junior hit .304, and led the league with 125 runs scored and 56 home runs, as well as a .646 slugging percentage and 393 total bases. He also led both leagues in runs batted in with 147.

His great season helped the Mariners to a 90-72 record, best in franchise history. Better yet, they won the American League West Division title by six games and were in the playoffs once again. The Mariners would have to play the Eastern Division champion Baltimore Orioles in the first round.

Unfortunately, the Mariners picked the wrong time to go into a team batting slump. After the Orioles defeated Randy Johnson and the Mariners 9-3 in the opening game at the Kingdome, the tone was set. Baltimore won the second game by an identical 9-3 score and were just one game away from clinching the best-of-five series.

Game three was in Baltimore, and the Mariners won. They took a 4-2 decision with Junior contributing an RBI single. But in the fourth game, Baltimore's

Mike Mussina outpitched Johnson, and the Orioles clinched the series by a 3-1 score. They had eliminated the Mariners in four games. There would be no World Series in Seattle in 1997.

Despite the playoff loss, Junior had yet another outstanding season. That was confirmed later when he was the unanimous choice for the American League's Most Valuable Player. It was the first time Junior had won that coveted prize.

"This award means a lot to me," said Junior. "Kids always think about being the MVP."

But he also went on to say that more meaningful to him was a World Series ring. "[Dad] asked me if I wanted to borrow his World Series ring," Junior said. "Hopefully, I'll get mine in '98."

Junior finished the 1997 season with 294 lifetime home runs. He was just 27 years old and would be entering his 10th season in 1998. By all indications, he had not yet reached his peak, and seemed to be getting better and better. Asked whether he thought he would play as long as his father had (19 years), Junior hesitated.

"A lot has to depend on my physical condition and what my family really needs from me," he said. "Money is not the thing that drives me. . . . I want to make sure that my family is taken care of. You know, once baseball's over, I've got to stay with them."

"I've got a three-year-old son and a baby daughter at home. After every game, [my son] rides with me back to the house and tells me what he did all day. Then I'll go tuck him into bed or we'll watch SportsCenter [on television]. I hope to give him the same values my father gave me."

It always seems to come back to family with the Griffeys. Ken Sr. has seen his son surpass him as a ballplayer. The senior Griffey was a fine player, perhaps an outstanding one. Junior is a superstar, a player well on his way to a place among the all-time greats. And that's just fine with his father.

Even with all his baseball achievements, Junior is proudest of his family. Here he poses with son Trey, wife Melissa, and daughter Taryn during family day at the Kingdome.

"I'm very, very proud of him, so proud you can't put it in words," Ken Sr. has said. "What I'm very happy about is what he does off the field, how he handles his fame and fortune."

As for Junior, the feeling is mutual. He feels he has gained much from the example his father set, both on and off the field.

"He was dad. He was cool," Junior said. "I owe him so much. I love him so much."

KEN GRIFFEY JR.: HIGHLIGHTS

1969   Born on November 21 in Donora, Pennsylvania.

1986   Leads his team to the Connie Mack League World Series.

1987   Graduates from Moeller High School in Cincinnati, Ohio, and is selected by the Seattle Mariners as the number-one draft choice.

       Is named to the all-league team in the Northwest League.

1989   Moves up to the Mariners' major-league club at the age of 19.

1990   On August 13, Ken Griffey Jr. and Ken Griffey Sr. become the first father-son pair to play on the same major-league team.

       Junior is voted to the American League All-Star Team and receives Gold Glove center fielder award.

1991   Receives second-straight Gold Glove award.

1992   Plays in third consecutive All-Star Game and is named Most Valuable Player of the game.

       Receives third Gold Glove award.

1993   Hits 45 home runs, with 180 hits and 109 runs batted in. Ties a major-league record with home runs in 8 consecutive games.

1994   In January, son Trey Kenneth Griffey is born.

       Becomes third-youngest player ever to reach 150 home-run mark. Finishes with 40 home runs, 90 RBIs, and .323 average.

1995   Mariners win 23 of last 30 games to finish first in their division and advance to playoffs for the first time.

       In October, daughter Taryn Kennedy Griffey is born.

1996   Sets team records with 49 home runs and 140 RBIs.

1997   Leads the American League with 56 home runs, 147 RBIs, and 125 runs scored.

       Leads Mariners to Western Division title and is named American League MVP.

FIND OUT MORE

Christopher, Matt. *At the Plate With Ken Griffey, Jr.* Boston: Little, Brown, 1997.

Joseph, Paul. *Ken Griffey, Jr.* Minneapolis: Abdo & Daughters, 1997.

Kramer, Barbara. *Ken Griffey, Jr.: All-Around Star*. Minneapolis: Lerner, 1996.

Sullivan, George. *Twenty-seven Exciting Stories About the Best Fielders in the History of Baseball*. New York: Simon and Schuster, 1996.

Weber, Bruce. *Baseball Megastars*. New York: Scholastic, 1997.

Websites:

Ken Griffey Jr.
http://www/uhu.com/junior/stats.html

Major League Baseball—Ken Griffey Jr.
http://www/majorleaguebaseball.com/bios/036269.sml

Seattle Mariners Home Plate
http://www.mariners.org/

How to write to Ken Griffey Jr.:
Ken Griffey Jr.
c/o Seattle Mariners
P.O. Box 4100
83 South King Street
Seattle, WA 98104

INDEX